MERRY WITCHMAS

By **Petrell Marie Özbay**
and **Tess La Bella**

Illustrated by **Sonya Abby**

BOYDS MILLS PRESS

AN IMPRINT OF BOYDS MILLS & KANE

New York

For Reina and Michael, who always believe in me —PMO

To my husband, Freddi, and our six beloved grandchildren—
Ethan, Max, Lily, Devin, Bella, and Teresina—with all my love —TL

To Mom, my sisters & brother, to Dad.
To Jonathan, Gigi, Sahara, and Stevee.
Thank you for believing in what I can do. —SA

Text copyright © 2021 by Petrell Marie Özbay and Tess La Bella
Illustrations copyright © 2021 by Sonya Abby
All rights reserved. Copying or digitizing this book for storage, display, or distribution
in any other medium is strictly prohibited.

For information about permission to reproduce selections from this book,
please contact permissions@bmkbooks.com.

Boyds Mills Press
An imprint of Boyds Mills & Kane, a division of Astra Publishing House
boydsmillspress.com
Printed in China

ISBN: 978-1-63592-318-6 (hc)
ISBN: 978-1-63592-469-5 (eBook)
Library of Congress Control Number: 2020947625

First edition
10 9 8 7 6 5 4 3 2 1

Design by Kate Gartner
The text is set in Chalkboard.
The title is set in Burton's Dream.
The illustrations are done digitally.

Ginger was like any other witch.
She wore a pointy hat.
She rode a magic broom.
She owned a black cat.

And she joked with
the neighborhood ghosts.

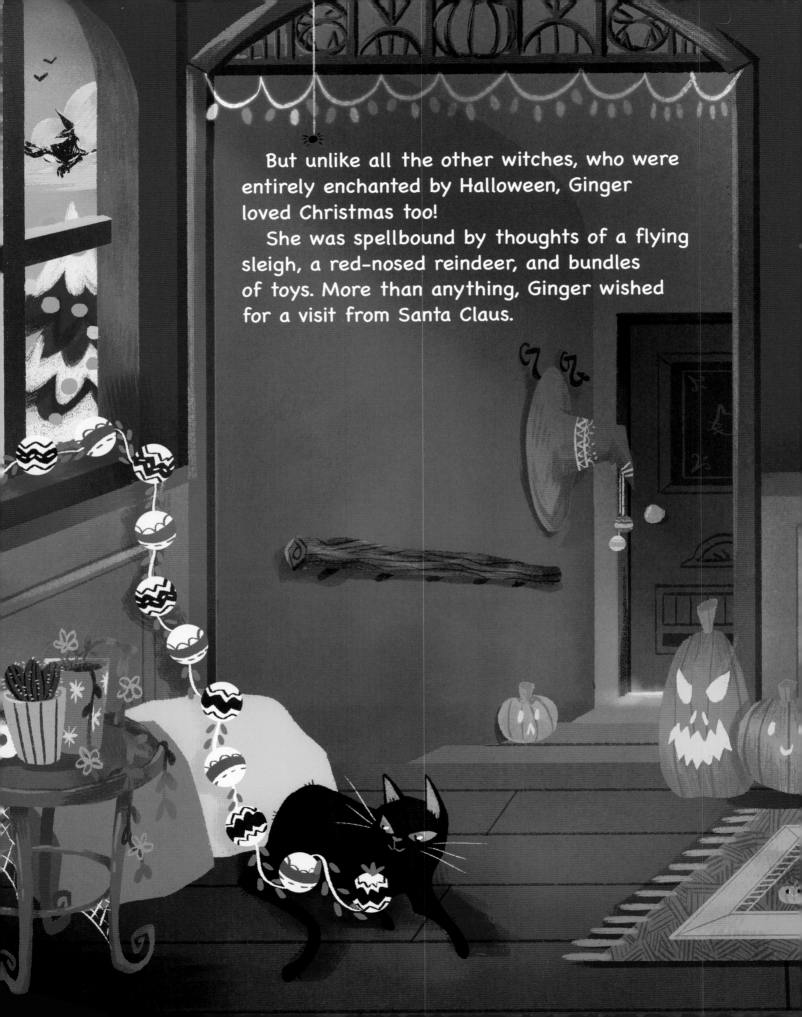

But unlike all the other witches, who were entirely enchanted by Halloween, Ginger loved Christmas too!

She was spellbound by thoughts of a flying sleigh, a red-nosed reindeer, and bundles of toys. More than anything, Ginger wished for a visit from Santa Claus.

So as soon as Halloween was over, for Ginger, the magic of Christmas began. Strands of jack-o'-lantern lights brightened her home. Striped stockings hovered near the mantel. The scent of gingerbread skeletons filled the air. Hot cocoa bubbled in her caldron.

And every Christmas season and throughout the year, Ginger worked to make it onto Santa's Nice List.

She fed stray black cats . . .

. . . and played hide-and-seek with neighborhood trolls.

She glued and painted broken broomsticks and mended hats for the elderly.

She tutored young witches and warlocks in spells.

Snowflurrious Fallifero

Still, even with Ginger's good deeds and endless Christmas cheer, she never got a single visit from Santa.

Ginger refused to give up. Determined to make this year her most holly jolly Christmas yet, she got out her sparkly markers and glitter glue.

Dear Santa,

I live in the Invisible Forest. If you don't believe in witches, my house is impossible to see. But I believe in you, so please believe in me. Love, Ginger

me →

Jingles ↓

P.S. I made you a MAP!

P.P.S. I'm including some leftover Halloween candy

P.P.P.S. I could really use a new broom!

my HOUSE!

With a wave of her wand . . .

The letter appeared on Santa's desk.
"Sweet Prancer!" Santa exclaimed.
"What's this?"

Upon reading the letter,
Santa picked up his Nice List.

"Hmmm . . . peppermint sticks! No witches named Ginger here," he said. He checked his Naughty List. He checked it twice. Ginger's name was nowhere to be found.

Santa was puzzled. He'd never believed in witches. So, quite simply, he never looked for them on Christmas Eve.

Could witches be real? he wondered, staring at the letter. "I guess if millions of kids believe in me, then I could believe in witches."

Although he wasn't quite sure, as Santa was filing
the letter away, he thought he saw the little
hand-drawn witch give a wink.

Santa chuckled and exclaimed, "Oh, by jingle!
Maybe witches are as real as Kris Kringle!"

On Christmas Eve, after Santa loaded up his sleigh, he kept one special package by his side.

Flying through the night sky, Santa was astonished to see haunted houses appearing right before his eyes—exactly where Ginger had directed him. The map in Santa's hand glowed just as he spied a twinkling house welcoming him to land.

When the sleigh touched down, the faint jingling of bells woke Ginger. "Santa?" Ginger gasped.

She tiptoed down the stairs
and peeked around the corner,
catching Santa's eye. Santa nodded
and smiled.

"Santa, it's really you!" exclaimed Ginger.

"Indeed, it is! And it's really you!" Santa marveled. "It sure took my jolly old self long enough to believe! Now, go have a look under that tree."

As Ginger unwrapped her very first
Christmas present, she cackled with delight.
"Sweepers, creepers! A Christmas broom!"

"I'd love to stay for milk and cookies, but there's no time to waste," declared Santa. "The world is waiting!"

"For the both of us!" said Ginger. "Race you up the chimney!"

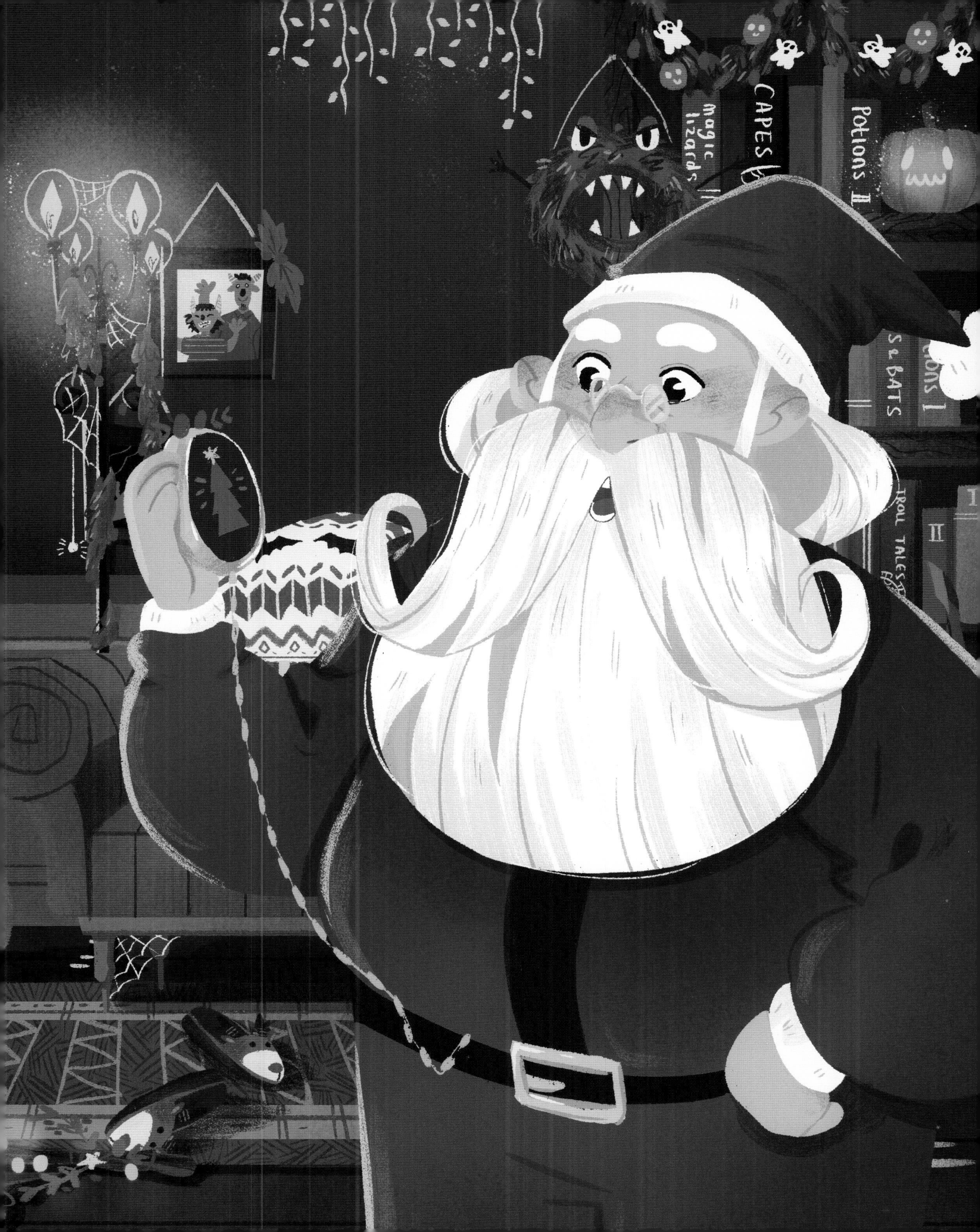
magic lizards
CAPES
Potions II
TROLL TALES

Up the chimney they rose. Soon Ginger soared among the stars, leading Santa's sleigh while the witches watched in wonder below.

"Well, Ginger," Santa said. "There's only one thing left to do. Would you like to do the honors?"

Bursting with joy, Ginger called out,

"MERRY WITCHMAS TO ALL,
AND TO ALL A GOOD NIGHT!"

12/22-1 (1/22)
9/23- 1(12/21)